For Oliver Thomas ~ P H

For Imogen, the new kid on the block ~ J L

LITTLE TIGER PRESS LTD,
an imprint of the Little Tiger Group
1 Coda Studios, 189 Munster Road, London SW6 6AW
Imported into the EEA by Penguin Random House Ireland,
Morrison Chambers, 32 Nassau Street, Dublin D02 YH68
www.littletiger.co.uk

First published in Great Britain 2020
This edition published 2021

Text by Patricia Hegarty
Text copyright © Little Tiger Press Ltd 2020
Illustrations copyright © Jonny Lambert 2020
Jonny Lambert has asserted his right to be identified as the illustrator
of this work under the Copyright, Designs and Patents Act, 1988
A CIP catalogue record for this book is available from the British Library

This Little Tiger book belongs to:

_____

_____

_____

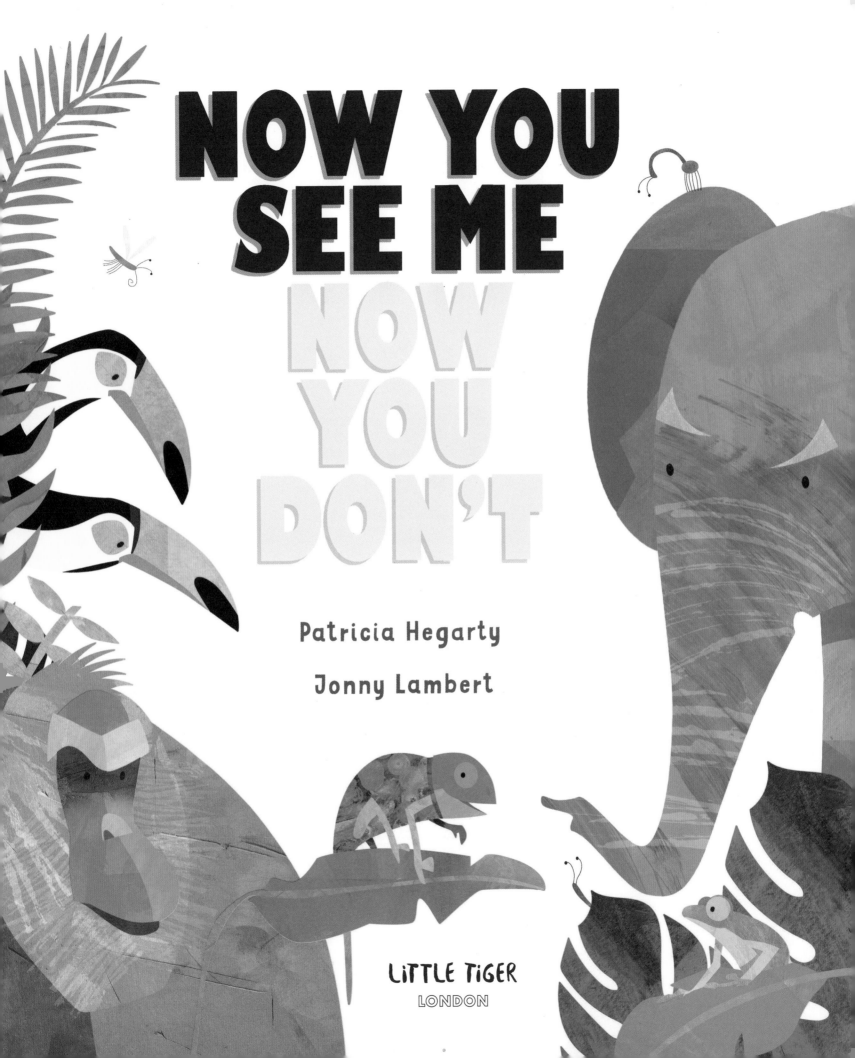

NOW YOU SEE ME
NOW YOU DON'T

Patricia Hegarty

Jonny Lambert

LITTLE TIGER

LONDON

I am **Chameleon**.
I do as I please.
I can play tricks
and nobody sees.

Just look at old **Big Ears**,
she thinks I'm a rock . . .

How do I do it?
It's **easy** as pie.

I can **change** colour
in the blink of an eye.

When work's to be done,
I just disappear.

Chores are for **bores**,
not for me – oh, **no fear!**

Bedtime's for losers,
not cool dudes like me.
It's hard to tuck in
a guy you **can't see!**

If I fancy a snack,
I just take my pick.
I **LOVE** a banana –
look at this trick!

There's fun to be had
with this **feathery** pair . . .

KWAAARK!

PLUCK!

I didn't do it!
I wasn't there!

I'm feeling INVINCIBLE!
Now what shall I do?
A sloth, fast asleep?
It's too good to be true!

TICKLE
TICKLE

Wheee! Down he goes,
with a bump and a lurch . . .
And bounces Anteater
right off of his perch.

Tee-hee, poor fellow,
look at him go!

He's going to land . . .

. . . on Jaguar!
UH-OH.

There's a horrified gasp
as all turn to see . . .
But Frog's disappeared –
all eyes are on ME!

Frog turned the tables
and now I can see:
It isn't so funny
when the joke is on me.

My camouflage tricks
are a thing of the past,
And everything's peaceful
in the jungle, at last . . .

But once in a while,
I just HAVE to go . . .

BOO!

So watch out, dear reader . . .
I might come for YOU!

More WILD ADVENTURES for little explorers . . .

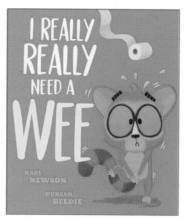
NIBBLES
THE DINOSAUR GUIDE
by EMMA YARLETT
DANGER

I REALLY REALLY NEED A WEE
KARL NEWSON
DUNCAN BEEDIE

LET'S ALL CREEP THROUGH CROCODILE CREEK
Jonny Lambert

The Monkey with a Bright Blue Bottom
STEVE SMALLMAN
NICK SCHON

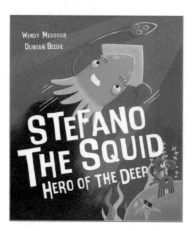
WENDY MEDDOUR
DUNCAN BEEDIE
STEFANO THE SQUID
HERO OF THE DEEP

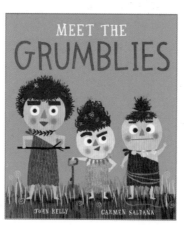
MEET THE GRUMBLIES
JOHN KELLY
CARMEN SALDAÑA

LiTTLE TiGER

For information regarding any of the above titles or for our catalogue, please contact us:
Little Tiger Press Ltd, 1 Coda Studios, 189 Munster Road, London SW6 6AW • Tel: 020 7385 6333
E-mail: contact@littletiger.co.uk • www.littletiger.co.uk